Speedy Flanagan, the shortest fast-ball pitcher in the Idaville Little League, walked into the Brown Detective Agency. He wore a face longer than the last day of school.

"I made a bet with Bugs Meany that Bugs couldn't get Spike Browning—the American League pitcher—to buy a secret pitch for a hundred dollars."

"Whoa!" cried Encyclopedia. "If I understand you, Bugs bet he could sell Spike Browning a special way to throw a baseball?"

"Right," said Speedy. "Bugs has a letter from Spike Browning and a check for a hundred dollars."

But when the boy detective saw the letter, he declared, "Spike Browning never wrote that letter. That check is a worthless piece of paper."

ENCYCLOPEDIA BROWN
and the Case of the Secret Pitch

"Most children like puzzles, and when they are presented as entertainingly as these are, they love them . . . Interest level is very high and the text is simple without being insulting."

—*Young Readers Review*

AMERICA'S SHERLOCK HOLMES IN SNEAKERS ★ No. 2 ★

ENCYCLOPEDIA BROWN
and the Case of the Secret Pitch

BY DONALD J. SOBOL

Illustrated by
Leonard Shortall

A BANTAM SKYLARK BOOK®
TORONTO • NEW YORK • LONDON • SYDNEY • AUCKLAND

For Betty and Tom Gentsch

*This low-priced Bantam Book
has been completely reset in a type face
designed for easy reading, and was printed
from new plates. It contains the complete
text of the original hard-cover edition.*

RL 3, 008-012

ENCYCLOPEDIA BROWN AND THE CASE OF THE SECRET PITCH

*A Bantam Skylark Book | published by arrangement with
Thomas Nelson Inc., Publishers*

PRINTING HISTORY

*Thomas Nelson edition published September 1965
10 printings through 1977*

Bantam Skylark edition | February 1978

2nd printing .... July 1978	8th printing ...... May 1980
3rd printing .. November 1978	9th printing ...... June 1980
4th printing .... May 1979	10th printing ...... July 1981
5th printing .... June 1979	11th printing .. February 1982
6th printing ... December 1979	12th printing ...... July 1982
7th printing .... May 1980	13th printing ...... July 1982

ISBN 0-553-15176-2

Published simultaneously in the United States and Canada

Bantam Books are published by Bantam Books, Inc. Its trademark, consisting of the words "Bantam Books" and the portrayal of a rooster, is Registered in U.S. Patent and Trademark Office and in other countries. Marca Registrada. Bantam Books, Inc., 666 Fifth Avenue, New York, New York 10103.

PRINTED IN THE UNITED STATES OF AMERICA

22   21   20   10   19   17

Contents

ENCYCLOPEDIA BROWN
and the Case of the Secret Pitch

The Case of the Secret Pitch

Idaville looked like any other town of its size—from the outside.

On the inside, however, it was different. Ten-year-old Encyclopedia Brown, America's Sherlock Holmes in sneakers, lived there.

Besides Encyclopedia, Idaville had three movie theaters, a Little League, four banks, and two delicatessens. It had large houses and small houses, good schools, churches, stores, and even an ugly old section by the railroad tracks.

And it had, everyone believed, the best police force in the world.

For more than a year no one—boy, girl,

or grown-up—had got away with breaking a single law.

Encyclopedia's father was chief of police. People said he was the smartest chief of police in the world and his officers were the best trained and the bravest. Chief Brown knew better.

His men were brave, true enough. They did their jobs well. But Chief Brown brought his hardest cases home for Encyclopedia to solve.

For a year now Chief Brown had been getting the answers during dinner in his red brick house on Rover Avenue. He never told a soul. How could he?

Who would believe that the guiding hand behind Idaville's crime cleanup wore a junior-size baseball mitt?

Encyclopedia never let out the secret, either. He didn't want to seem different from other fifth-graders.

There was nothing he could do about his nickname, however.

An encyclopedia is a book or set of books filled with facts on all subjects. Encyclopedia had read so many books his head held more facts than a library.

Nobody but his teachers and his parents

called him by his real name, Leroy. He was called Encyclopedia by everyone else in Idaville.

Encyclopedia did not do all his crime-busting seated at the dinner table. During the summer he usually solved mysteries while walking around.

Soon after vacation began, he had opened his own detective business. He wanted to help others.

Children seeking help of every kind came to his office in the Brown garage.

Encyclopedia handled each case himself. The terms of his business were clearly stated on the sign that hung outside the garage.

One morning Speedy Flanagan, the shortest fast-ball pitcher in the Idaville Little League, walked into the Brown Detective Agency. He wore a face longer than the last day of school.

"I need help," he said, side-arming twenty-five cents onto the gasoline can beside Encyclopedia. "What do you know about Browning?"

"Nothing, I've never browned," replied Encyclopedia. "But once at the beach I tanned something awful, and—"

"I mean Robert Browning," said Speedy.

"The English poet?"

"No, no," said Speedy. "The American League pitcher, Robert *Spike* Browning."

Even Encyclopedia's Aunt Bessie knew of Spike Browning. He was the ace of the New York Yankees' pitching staff.

"What do you want to know about him?" asked Encyclopedia.

"Do you know what his handwriting looks like?" asked Speedy. "I made a bet

with Bugs Meany—my bat against his—
that Bugs couldn't get Spike Browning to
buy a secret pitch for a hundred dollars."

"Whoa!" cried Encyclopedia. "If I understand you, Bugs bet he could sell Spike
Browning a special way to throw a baseball?"

"Right. Bugs and his father were in New
York City the last week in June," said
Speedy. "Bugs says he sold Spike Brown-
ing his cross-eyed special."

"You'd better explain," said Encyclopedia.

"The pitcher crosses his eyes whenever
there are runners on first and third bases,"
said Speedy. "That way nobody knows
where he's looking—whether he's going to
throw to first base, third base, or home
plate. The runners don't dare take a lead.
The secret is how the pitcher can throw the
ball some place while staring himself in
the eye. Bugs sold the secret. He has a letter from Spike Browning and a check for a
hundred dollars!"

"Phew!" said Encyclopedia. "I understand you now. You figure Bugs wrote the
letter and the check himself to win the bet
and your bat. So do I! Let's go see Bugs."

Bugs Meany was the leader of the Tigers, a gang of older boys who caused more trouble than itching powder in Friday's wash. Since setting up as a detective, Encyclopedia had stopped many of Bug's shady deals.

The Tigers' clubhouse was a tool shed behind Mr. Sweeny's Auto Body Shop. When Encyclopedia and Speedy arrived, Bugs was leading a discussion on how to beat the bubble gum machines around town.

The Tigers' leader broke off to greet Encyclopedia. "Get lost," he said.

"Not until I have a chance to see the letter and check from Spike Browning," said Encyclopedia.

Bugs opened a cigar box and passed Encyclopedia a check and a letter. Encyclopedia read the letter.

Yankee Stadium, New York
June 31

Dear Bugs:

Your cross-eyed pitch is the greatest thing since the spitball. I expect to win thirty games with it this season.

For sole rights to the secret of it, I'm

Bugs grinned as Encyclopedia read the letter.

happy to enclose my check for one hundred dollars.

Yours truly,

Spike Browning

The letter was written on plain white paper. The check, bearing the same date as the letter, was drawn on the First National Bank for one hundred dollars.

"Spike will win fifty games this season," said Bugs. "And I won one baseball bat from Speedy Flanagan. So where is it?"

"Where's *your* bat?" corrected Encyclopedia. "Speedy won the bet. You lost. The letter and check are fakes."

"I ought to shove those words down your throat," said Bugs. "But I'm feeling too good about what I did for the great American game of baseball."

Bugs crossed his eyes. Humming to himself, he went into his secret throwing motion. The other Tigers cheered wildly.

"Man, oh man!" sang Bugs. "I invented the greatest pitch since Edison threw out the gas lamp. No smart-aleck private detective is going to walk in here and call me a liar!"

"Oh, yes I am," said Encyclopedia.

"Spike Browning never wrote that letter. That check is a worthless piece of paper!"

WHAT MADE ENCYCLOPEDIA SO CERTAIN?

(Turn to page 103 for the solution to The Case of the Secret Pitch.)

The Case of the Balloon Man

"Leroy!" Mrs. Brown called. "Leroy, it's time for dinner. Wash up, please."

Encyclopedia put down the book he was reading, *Six Ways to Reach the Moon on a Budget*. In the bathroom he gave his face a lick and a promise.

When he got to the table, his father looked at him in a strange way.

"Do you know Bobby Tyler?" Chief Brown asked his only child.

"Sure," said Encyclopedia. "He was in my homeroom last year. Did anything happen to him, Dad?"

"He's missing," said Chief Brown.

"You mean he ran away from home?"

Chief Brown shook his head.

Encyclopedia gasped. Mrs. Brown stopped in the kitchen doorway, her eyes opened wide.

"*Kidnapped?*" mother and son asked together.

"It looks that way," answered Chief Brown.

"Do you know who took Bobby?" asked Mrs. Brown.

"Yes, Izzy the balloon man."

"Izzy?" cried Encyclopedia. "No, Dad. Izzy couldn't do anything so terrible!"

"What do you know about Izzy?" asked Chief Brown gently. "Do you know what kind of man he *really* is? Do you even know where he lives?"

"I know he loves children," insisted Encyclopedia. "Otherwise he wouldn't do what he does for a living."

"He has an old truck and sells ice cream, candy, and soda, mostly to children," Chief Brown explained to his wife.

"Why is he called the balloon man?" she asked.

"If you buy more than seventy cents worth of candy or anything, he gives you a green and pink balloon free," answered Encyclopedia.

"I guess Izzy got tired of blowing up balloons," said Chief Brown quietly. "Bobby's father is wealthy. So Izzy—"

"I don't believe it!" exclaimed Encyclopedia. "You ought to see Izzy stick the end of a balloon in his mouth and huff and puff like a steam engine till it's blown up. He always makes funny faces so the kids will laugh."

"All right, son," said Chief Brown. "I'll accept three facts. One, Izzy is a funny fellow who always blows up balloons with his mouth for laughs. Two, children love him and he loves children. And three, Sam Potts saw him kidnap little Bobby Tyler this afternoon."

"There was an eyewitness?" Encyclopedia asked.

"Mr. Potts came down to headquarters when he heard little Bobby was missing. He gave me a complete statement," said Chief Brown. "I made some notes to bring home to you. Want to hear them?"

Encyclopedia closed his eyes as he always did before using his brain at full power. "Go ahead, Dad."

Chief Brown took his notebook from his breast pocket. He looked it over a moment.

Then he repeated what Mr. Potts had told him.

"This morning Izzy made a stop near Bobby Tyler's house and drove off—or so it appeared," Chief Brown began. "Later Sam Potts and Reverend Bevin were in Sam's back yard, which is right behind the Tylers' walled back yard.

"Sam saw a green and pink balloon—the kind Izzy gives away—rise into his oak tree," continued Chief Brown. "The balloon stuck high among the branches. Because there was no breeze to blow the balloon loose, Sam got a long ladder and climbed into the tree."

Chief Brown paused as he turned over a page in his notebook. He went on.

"From up in the tree, Sam could see over the Tylers' twelve-foot wall. Sam says that as he freed the balloon, he looked down in the Tylers' yard. He saw Izzy put Bobby into his truck and drive off. Sam told Reverend Bevin what he had just seen. Both men took it for granted that Bobby's mother had said he could go for a ride in Izzy's truck. Later, when the Reverend learned that Bobby was missing, he advised Sam Potts to see me."

Sam climbed into the tree.

Chief Brown closed his notebook.

"An hour after Sam Potts had told me what he had seen, Bobby's father telephoned. He had received a note. It said he must pay sixty thousand dollars or never see Bobby again. He would learn where to leave the money tomorrow."

Chief Brown stopped talking. Both he and Mrs. Brown looked at Encyclopedia.

Idaville's ace detective kept his eyes closed in thought a long time after his father had finished talking.

At last he opened his eyes. He asked two questions—it seldom took more than two to solve a mystery when his father gave him the facts.

"How does Mr. Potts earn his living?" he asked first.

His father frowned. "Why, I don't know. He's only been in Idaville two months. He doesn't own the house behind the Tylers'. He just rents it."

Encyclopedia's second question was, "Did Reverend Bevin see the balloon fly into the tree?"

"No," said his father. "But Sam Potts did, and the Reverend saw it stuck in the branches. What difference does the balloon make?"

"It solves the case," answered Encyclopedia.

"Do you know where Bobby is?" asked his mother anxiously. "Is he unhurt?"

"I don't know that, Mom," said Encyclopedia, realizing that he had spoken too quickly. "But I know who kidnapped Bobby."

"We already know that," pointed out Chief Brown. "It was Izzy the balloon man."

"No, Izzy has probably been kidnapped too," said Encyclopedia.

Chief Brown sat back and stared.

"The guilty man," said Encyclopedia, "had to find someone to blame Bobby's kidnapping on. Izzy was chosen. So Izzy has to be kept hidden or he'll deny the crime."

"What makes you so all-fire certain Izzy didn't kidnap Bobby Tyler?" demanded Chief Brown.

"Because Mr. Potts kidnapped Bobby," answered Encyclopedia.

"Sam Potts may be a stranger in Idaville, but that doesn't make him a kidnapper," said Chief Brown angrily. "And don't forget Reverend Bevin was right there with him."

"Mr. Potts wanted him there," said Encyclopedia. "The Reverend was a perfect witness. But the Reverend couldn't see over the wall into Bobby's back yard. He had to accept what Mr. Potts, up in the tree, *said* he saw."

"Are you telling me that Sam Potts used the Reverend?" said Chief Brown.

"He did," said Encyclopedia.

"I'm sorry, son," said Chief Brown. "You just don't have any reason for saying Mr. Potts lied about seeing Izzy put Bobby into his truck."

"I have a very good reason, Dad," said Encyclopedia. "Mr. Potts might have got away with the kidnapping and collected the sixty thousand dollars ransom. But he overlooked one simple fact about Izzy!"

WHAT HAD MR. POTTS
OVERLOOKED?

*(Turn to page 104 for the solution to
The Case of the Balloon Man.)*

The Case of
the Ambushed Cowboy

Through his detective agency, Encyclopedia solved cases for children of the neighborhood. Occasionally he even solved cases for grown-ups. Whether his customers were children or grown-ups, they had one thing in common.

They were always alive.

He never supposed that one day he would solve a case in which all the people had been dead for nearly one hundred years.

But that is what he did—twice—while on a trip out West.

The two adventures in long-range detec-

tive work had their beginnings in the
Brown dining room. The dinner hour was
very quiet. For the third straight evening
Chief Brown had not brought home a mystery for Encyclopedia to solve.

There was nothing to do but eat.

"It's time we took a vacation," said Mrs.
Brown.

Chief Brown agreed. "I haven't taken
any time off in three years," he said. "We
could go on a long trip."

"Let's go to Texas," suggested Encyclo-
pedia. He had just read a book called
*Upper Cretaceous Limestone in the Lone
Star State*.

"It certainly is a long way from Idaville,"
said Mrs. Brown. And as nobody could ad-
vance a better reason for going to Texas,
she began at once to make plans.

Two weeks later Encyclopedia found
himself bouncing painfully atop an
honest-to-goodness Texas mustang. His
father was riding right in front of him. The
boy detective wished he had stayed behind his mother instead. She had ridden a
taxi into Fort Worth to have lunch and
shop for gifts.

Since sunrise Encyclopedia, his father,
and fourteen fellow guests at the Badlands

Inn had been in the saddle. They had paid
five dollars each for this tour of "Historic
Scenes of the Old Wild West."

"All right, folks, dismount!" shouted Mr.
Scotty, the tour's skinny little guide.

Mr. Scotty had bowlegs. They made Encyclopedia think of rain.

"I could open an umbrella between Mr.
Scotty's knees and never touch either
one," Encyclopedia thought.

Mr. Scotty pointed to a high rock that
formed a perfect corner.

"That there is the Johnny Kid corner,"
he said. "Back in the eighteen-seventies,
Johnny Kid ambushed Ringo Charlie on
that very spot."

The members of the tour stepped forward. They looked at the rock. They
looked at Mr. Scotty.

Mr. Scotty spat tobacco juice between
his teeth.

"In them days," he said, "Johnny Kid
and Ringo Charlie were feuding at the
poker table. Johnny Kid claimed Ringo
Charlie kept too many extra cards up his
sleeve. Johnny Kid never complained very
loud, though. Ringo Charlie was cousin to
half the townsfolk, and he was said to be
the fastest draw in Texas."

Mr. Scotty walked toward the high rock.

"One fine day," he went on, "Johnny Kid got fed up with losing money to a sixty-card deck. So he hid behind this here rock and waited his chance."

Mr. Scotty then acted out what Johnny Kid had done so long ago. He crouched behind the high rock.

"Along about this time of morning—nine o'clock," Mr. Scotty continued, "Ringo Charlie comes riding along."

Here the skinny guide rose from his crouch. He rounded the stone corner and turned and started back toward it. Now he was acting out the part of Ringo Charlie.

As Mr. Scotty moved toward the corner, he squinted into the morning sun. One hand was cupped above where a pistol would hang at his hip.

Encyclopedia could almost see Johnny Kid crouched behind the rock, waiting in ambush. Mr. Scotty was Ringo Charlie riding toward him, unaware.

Mr. Scotty picked up the tale again.

"Johnny Kid saw Ringo Charlie's shadow coming while Ringo Charlie was still on the other side of the rock. Out jumps Johnny Kid from behind the rock, both guns blazing. Ringo Charlie is hit. But

The skinny guide acted out the part.

his horse breaks into a gallop and carries him back to town."

Mr. Scotty squirted more tobacco juice. He hit a lizard between the eyes.

"Ringo Charlie," he said, "told the townsfolk what had happened. A fair fight was one thing, but Johnny Kid had taken foul advantage of poor Ringo Charlie, and Ringo Charlie was cousin to half the town."

Mr. Scotty stopped talking. He started toward his horse. It was a nice effect. A fat man in a yellow shirt cried, "Well, what happened?"

"Why," said Mr. Scotty, turning, "Ringo Charlie's cousins chased Johnny Kid clear into Oklahoma!"

"They should have caught and hanged him!" exclaimed the fat man.

"If they had," spoke up Encyclopedia, "they'd have hanged an innocent man."

"Wh-what's that you say, boy?" gasped Mr. Scotty.

"Ringo Charlie lied about the shooting," said Encyclopedia.

Mr. Scotty nearly swallowed his tobacco. "Why?"

"I guess he hated to admit he'd been

beaten by Johnny Kid in a gun fight," replied Encyclopedia.

"Appears like you're a right smart young fellow," said Mr. Scotty. "Now tell me how you can know so much about something that happened eighty-five years ago?"

"Whether it happened then or yesterday wouldn't make any difference," said Encyclopedia. "Ringo Charlie can't lie about the laws of nature!"

HOW DID ENCYCLOPEDIA KNOW RINGO CHARLIE HAD LIED ABOUT THE SHOOTING?

(Turn to page 105 for the solution to The Case of the Ambushed Cowboy.)

The Case of
the Forgetful Sheriff

Led by Mr. Scotty, the party of eastern tourists rode the Texas range. The hotel manager had promised them "Historic Scenes of the Old Wild West." Who knew what another mile might bring?

Encyclopedia Brown knew. More blisters.

He rode last in line. Behind him came only the chuck wagon with the food. Around noon, even the chuck wagon passed him.

Encyclopedia didn't mind. It was lunch time.

Most of the tourists (including Encyclopedia) ate standing up. It made the boy detective mad to see his father sitting contentedly on the ground.

"You don't look well, Leroy," he said.

"I wish Bugs Meany were sitting in my place," said Encyclopedia.

Chief Brown grinned. "I had the cowboy at the hotel give you the gentlest horse in the stable."

"Then I must have the toughest saddle," answered Encyclopedia. "Say, Dad, do you think I made Mr. Scotty mad before?"

"No, but you upset him when you figured out the truth about the gunfight between Ringo Charlie and Johnny Kid," replied his father.

"I'll try to keep still," vowed Encyclopedia.

For the next half hour of riding there was little else to do. The horses plodded across flat grasslands. At last Mr. Scotty called, "Dismount here, folks."

The skinny little guide led the way to a pocket formed by nine high rocks.

"Now this here spot is called Outlaw Cemetery. It was so named on account of the five outlaws done in here eighty years ago," he began.

"Them outlaws held up the bank at

River Falls. They escaped with twelve thousand dollars in gold," said Mr. Scotty.

"Sheriff Wiggins immediately set out after the desperadoes. But he was new on the job and forgetful. He forgot to put on his six-gun."

Mr. Scotty paused. He looked at the crowd of tourists to see if everyone was paying attention. He looked especially at Encyclopedia.

Then he resumed his tale.

"One of the citizens of River Falls happened to enter the sheriff's office. He saw the sheriff's six-gun still on the desk. Quickly he spread the word. A posse of citizens was rounded up to ride out and help the unarmed lawman capture the bank robbers. About ten miles out of town the posse heard gun play. When the shooting stopped, the posse rode up to this here spot. Stretched out dead as fish in a barrel were them five outlaws."

Mr. Scotty began hopping about as he warmed to his tale.

"Sheriff Wiggins," he said, "had recovered the stolen gold. But he was wounded in his left arm. In his modest way, he told the posse what had happened.

He said the lookout for the outlaws saw him coming and shot two bullets into his left arm."

Suddenly Mr. Scotty clutched his left arm above the elbow. Then he made a leap and began to throw himself around.

"Sheriff Wiggins said he wrested the lookout's pearl-handled six-gun away despite his wounded left arm. Then he shot the lookout with his own gun—a bullet through the heart it was."

At this point, Mr. Scotty dropped to one knee. "Right away the other four outlaws came at Sheriff Wiggins shooting up a storm," he said. "But the sheriff was cool as a hog on ice. He drilled them four desperadoes—*bang! bang! bang! bang!* in four seconds flat."

The skinny little guide jumped to his feet. He was breathing heavily with the effort of acting out the heroic sheriff's one-man stand against the five outlaws.

"The outlaws were buried on boothill," he continued. "The stolen gold was returned to the bank at River Falls. Everybody in town claimed Sheriff Wiggins ought to run for President."

Mr. Scotty dusted himself off carefully,

Mr. Scotty clutched his left arm.

letting the tourists wait for more of the story.

Then he said, "The town gave a dinner for the sheriff, though he said he didn't deserve the honor. Why, he was only doing his duty getting back the stolen gold, he said. But Mr. Baker, the bank president, disagreed."

Again Mr. Scotty broke off his tale to look at the tourists. He shot Encyclopedia a sly glance. It seemed to say, "Ready to solve this one, sonny?"

"Mr. Baker," concluded Mr. Scotty, "said Sheriff Wiggins had done a mite more than his duty. And since this was the lawman's last meal, he'd better eat well. Then Mr. Baker said something that made the three biggest men at the dinner seize Sheriff Wiggins. Somebody got a rope, and at sunrise they hanged the lawman!"

The tourists gasped in amazement.

After a brief silence, a lady from Vermont asked, "What did Mr. Baker say that made them hang the sheriff?"

"Why, now, that's the puzzle, isn't it?" replied Mr. Scotty. "I don't expect that anybody here could solve it, could he?"

The skinny little guide did not mention

anyone by name. But the grown-ups on the tour turned and looked at Encyclopedia.

Chief Brown looked at him, too.

"Should I speak out, Dad?" asked Encyclopedia.

"If you know what Mr. Baker said that made the citizens hang Sheriff Wiggins," said his father.

Encyclopedia took a step forward. "Mr. Baker said that—"

WHAT DID MR. BAKER SAY?

(Turn to page 106 for the solution to The Case of the Forgetful Sheriff.)

The Case of
the Hungry Hitchhiker

Encyclopedia had a good time in Texas. But for many days after his return to Idaville he did not ride his bike. It felt too much like a horse.

In the mornings he used his brains to solve cases in the Brown garage. Afternoons he used his feet. Usually he walked down to Mill Creek and fished with some of the gang—Billy and Jody Turner, Pinky Plummer, Herb Stein, Charlie Stewart, and Sally Kimball.

On very hot evenings Chief Brown drove by Mill Creek and gave Encyclopedia a lift home.

"Boy, this feels great," said Encyclopedia one evening as he climbed into the air-conditioned patrol car. "It must be ninety degrees out."

"Ninety-three," said his father.

Just then the police radio blared.

Sergeant Murphy's voice spoke from headquarters. He announced the news of a holdup.

The First Federal Savings and Loan Association had been held up ten minutes ago. The four masked bandits had escaped in a blue sedan. The car was last seen racing north on National Highway.

Sergeant Murphy signed off. Immediately Encyclopedia's father picked up the two-way speaker.

"This is Chief Brown," he said. "I'm at the corner of Mill and Commerce streets. I'll go directly to National Highway. Send cars four and five out by the Midland road. Also, telephone the police in Allentown, Mooresville, and Devon Hills. Have them be on the lookout for the getaway car."

Chief Brown put back the speaker. He swung the car about and speeded up.

Encyclopedia could feel his heart beating faster. He had never been on a real cops-and-robbers chase before.

"We can't overtake them," said his father. "They have too big a head start. I'm hoping that somebody saw what road they took."

Chief Brown steered onto National Highway. He drove north, the direction the holdup men were reported to have taken.

Ahead, Encyclopedia made out a hitchhiker standing at the crossroads of the highway and Coconut Drive. He was a young man with a knapsack over one shoulder.

"If the getaway car passed this way, that hitchhiker must have seen it," said Encyclopedia.

"He may have," replied Chief Brown. "It would depend on how long he has been standing there."

Chief Brown braked to a stop beside the hitchhiker.

"How long have you been standing here?" he asked.

"About an hour," answered the hitchhiker.

"Did a blue car with four or five men in it speed past you?"

"It sure did," said the hitchhiker. "It came from the same way you did and turned here. Gosh, it nearly ran me down.

Chief Brown braked to a stop.

Those fellows were in a mighty big hurry!"

"You'd better climb in," said Chief Brown.

The hitchhiker stared at Chief Brown's uniform. "Gosh," he said. "Is it against the law to hitchhike? Are you taking me to jail?"

"Climb in," said Chief Brown. "Don't worry. I want you as a witness. If we catch up with a blue car, could you tell whether the driver was the same one who nearly ran you down?"

"Yes, I'd know his face," said the hitchhiker, getting into the back seat.

As Chief Brown sped the engine, he talked over the two-way radio again.

"Murphy, I'm heading east on Coconut Drive," he said. "Have the Allentown police stop all cars. We might catch the holdup men before they leave the state."

In the back seat the hitchhiker had opened his knapsack.

"Care for an orange?" he asked Encyclopedia. "Or a piece of chocolate?"

"Can I have a piece of chocolate, Dad?" asked Encyclopedia.

"You'll ruin your dinner, but this is not exactly the time to talk about it," said Chief Brown. "Go ahead."

Encyclopedia took the chocolate bar from the hitchhiker. He broke off two squares and handed back the rest.

The hitchhiker put the candy into his knapsack. He got out an orange and began to peel it. He put the peels neatly into a paper bag.

Encyclopedia moved the chocolate under his tongue. He hardly tasted it because suddenly he was scared.

He dug into his pocket and came up with a stub of a pencil. There was nothing to write on, however.

"Dad, could I have another piece of chocolate?" he asked.

His father nodded. The hitchhiker gave a friendly laugh and passed over the candy bar.

Encyclopedia popped the chocolate into his mouth. Slowly and carefully, so the hitchhiker couldn't see, he spread the wrapper on his leg. He wrote:

"Hitchhiker is member of holdup gang."

Then he worked the paper over the front seat till it was on his father's lap. His father glanced down and then returned his gaze to the road.

A few minutes later they reached Allentown. Chief Brown opened the door as though he merely wanted to stretch his legs.

All at once he was around by the back door. He had his pistol out, and he pointed the muzzle at the hitchhiker.

"We missed your partners, but we've got you," he said grimly. "And you'll tell us all we need to know about the holdup."

HOW DID ENCYCLOPEDIA KNOW THE HITCHHIKER WAS A MEMBER OF THE HOLDUP GANG?

(Turn to page 107 for the solution to The Case of the Hungry Hitchhiker.)

The Case of
the Two-Fisted Poet

Encyclopedia kept the money he earned from his detective business in a shoe box. He hid the shoe box behind an old tire in the garage.

That wasn't the best place to keep money. Still, it was better than keeping shoes there.

Every Friday after lunch Sally Kimball came by. Together they took the week's earnings to the bank. Sally was Idaville's best fighter under twelve years of age. Encyclopedia had made her his bodyguard and junior partner.

As Encyclopedia waited for Sally one Friday, a boy rode up on a bike. His hair was too long and his clothes were too tight. He wore eyeglasses, shiny black shoes, and a *necktie*.

The boy stopped to read Encyclopedia's business sign outside the garage. "A poem," he announced out of the air.

"Huh?" said Encyclopedia.

Ignoring Encyclopedia, the boy on the bike uttered:

> *Roses are red,*
> *Violets are blue,*
> *You can't solve cases*
> *Without a clue!*

The boy smiled as though he'd just finished delivering *The Song of Hiawatha* straight from memory. He bowed to the sign and rode away.

"Sa-a-ay," said Encyclopedia when Sally arrived. "You should have seen what went on here a minute ago. That new kid— what's his name?"

"Percy Arbuthnot?"

"Yes, Percy," said Encyclopedia. "He recited a poem. I swear he made it up on the spot!"

"Percy is very smart," said Sally. "He went to school in England."

"Good for him," said Encyclopedia. "Now let's get to the bank."

"I'm not going," said Sally. "Being a bodyguard isn't ladylike."

"Who told you that?" asked Encyclopedia.

"Percy," replied Sally. "When he learned I once flattened Bugs Meany, he was horrified. He told me to stop acting like a common tomboy. So I'm quitting."

"Idaville," mumbled Encyclopedia, "can get along without Percy."

"He's a gentleman," said Sally. "He's taking me to see *Gone With the Wind* tonight in a taxicab. You can bet he won't be wearing sneakers!"

Sally tilted up her nose, spun on her heel, and strode from the garage.

Encyclopedia forgot about going to the bank. He sat down to think over the problem of Percy Arbuthnot.

He decided to visit the scene of the crime.

As he got off his bike that evening near the movie theater, he kept a sharp lookout for a taxicab. One pulled to the curb two blocks away. Percy got out and then helped Sally to alight. They walked toward the movie theater holding hands.

"He doesn't miss a trick," Encyclopedia thought glumly. "He's got better manners than a French waiter. But why did they get out of the taxicab so far from the theater?"

As Encyclopedia watched, a big boy stepped from the shadows. He bumped squarely into Percy.

Encyclopedia couldn't hear what was being said, but Percy and the big boy began to argue. The big boy was about sixteen, broad, and a head taller than Percy.

Encyclopedia hurried over to stop a possible murder. As he got close, he heard Percy declare:

"My dear chap. Unless you take back what you have just said, I shall be forced to box your ears."

"Listen to the canary kid, will you?" jeered the big boy.

"Tut, tut," said Percy. Calmly he took off his eyeglasses and placed them in the breast pocket of his blue suitcoat.

"A poem," he announced, and forthwith launched into:

> You call me names,
> My strength you doubt,
> So pardon me
> While I knock you out!

The big boy's jaw dropped open in surprise. Percy closed it with an uppercut.

Thereupon both boys fell to pounding each other with body blows to the chest and stomach. Percy mixed poetry and punches with a fearlessness that amazed Encyclopedia. After the second poem and the umpteenth punch, the big boy had enough. He took to his heels.

Triumphantly, Percy put on his eyeglasses and combed his hair.

Sally gazed at him with shining eyes—till Encyclopedia whispered into her ear.

The look in Sally's eyes changed from hero-worship to anger.

"Percy, y-you phoney!" she cried. "You fixed that fight. It wasn't a real fight at all!"

"How dare you say such a thing," retorted Percy, sniffing. "Upon my honor, if you were a boy, I'd bash you good and proper."

"Forget I'm a girl," snapped Sally. She reached out and gave his nose a twist.

That did it. Percy lost his temper.

He snorted free, whipped off his eyeglasses, and struck a fighting pose.

"You asked for this!" he bawled.

The fight was short and sweet. Percy had no chance to slip in any poetry licks. He

Sally reached out and gave his nose a twist.

spent his time going down and getting up.

At last Sally put him down for keeps. "Phoney!" she said, and marched off in a swirl of skirts.

Percy lay on the sidewalk with his eyes closed. For a long time he did not move. Encyclopedia grew worried.

"Percy, say something!" he begged.

"Is she gone?" said Percy.

"Yes," Encyclopedia assured him. "You're safe."

Percy opened one eye. "A poem," he moaned:

> *What was the mistake*
> *I made tonight*
> *Trying to show off*
> *How well I fight?*

WHAT MISTAKE OF PERCY'S HAD ENCYCLOPEDIA POINTED OUT TO SALLY?

(Turn to page 108 for the solution to The Case of the Two-Fisted Poet.)

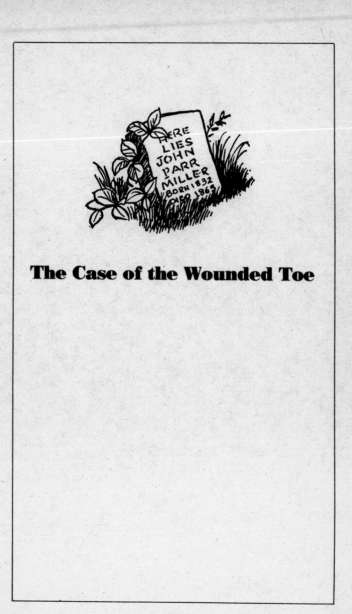

The Case of the Wounded Toe

Charlie Stewart had the biggest tooth collection of any boy in Idaville.

After every rain, he went off tooth-hunting. Encyclopedia frequently went with him.

"The rain water washes off the dirt," explained Charlie. "Sometimes you can see an opossum's tooth shining fifty feet away."

Charlie didn't depend entirely upon the rain to help him find interesting teeth. He was more scientific. He took off his shoes.

"Shoes cut down your chances," said Charlie. "With shoes on, you can step on a partly buried tooth without feeling it. But if you go barefoot, you get bitten sort of."

Off came his shoes. He tied them together by the laces and hung them about his neck.

He began wiggling his toes. In a few minutes he was warmed up. "Okay, I'm ready," he said. "Let's get started."

The two friends planned to search in a new area. They entered the woods near Mill Creek and walked northward.

This way they could avoid the garbage dump. But they would have to pass close to the ancient burial grounds in order to end up at Charlie's house.

"I used to spend a lot of time in the garbage dump," said Charlie. "But all I ever took away were sore feet. Did you ever get a toe stuck in an old dishwasher?"

"No, I can't honestly say that I ever did," answered Encyclopedia. "Once I caught my hand in a bed I was making. I had my mind on a case."

The two boys moved slowly through the woods, their eyes searching the ground.

After a mile Charlie found two raccoon teeth. He threw them away. He already had a complete set.

Encyclopedia found a few bottle caps, an old tennis ball, and a last month's newspaper. Then, near the ancient burial grounds, he found something worth keeping.

He found a felt hat—like those worn by Bugs Meany and his Tigers.

"What do you suppose the Tigers were doing way out here?" wondered Encyclopedia.

"I don't know," said Charlie. "And I don't care. This place gives me the spooks. Let's go."

Encyclopedia stared over the rusty fence. Weeds had overgrown the graves. Wild vines twisted around the small tombstones, which bore the names of early settlers and soldiers.

Encyclopedia pointed to a tree near the fence. Nailed to the trunk was a red and white target.

"Come back!" hollered Charlie as Encyclopedia climbed the rusty fence. "It's against the law to go inside the ancient burial grounds."

"I'm only going to sit on the fence," said Encyclopedia. "Now get on my shoulders. Take a close look at that target."

"Not me," said Charlie. "I could fall in

"Now take a close look at that target."

there." Nevertheless, he did as Encyclopedia bid him.

He put his nose close to the target. "Somebody's been doing a lot of shooting with an air gun," he called. "The bull's eye is filled with pellets."

"Hmmm," said Encyclopedia. "Come on down."

As Charlie landed, he let out a yelp. He rolled on the ground moaning, "My foot, my foot."

Suddenly he sat up, as if struck by a happy thought. "Maybe I was bit by a buffalo tooth," he said hopefully.

Encyclopedia knelt beside the tooth hunter. He wiped the blood from his friend's left foot with a clean handkerchief.

"W-why," Encyclopedia gasped in astonishment. "You've been shot! There's a little pellet in your big toe. Does it hurt much?"

"Not much," said Charlie. "But the longer we stay around this place, the worse I feel."

Encyclopedia helped Charlie to his feet and out of the woods.

Ten minutes later Charlie's mother watched anxiously as Dr. Ross removed the pellet from her son's toe.

"Do you know who shot you?" asked the doctor.

"We have a clue," answered Charlie. "Encyclopedia found a hat—the kind all the Tigers wear. We think one of them shot me."

"Stay away from those boys," said Charlie's mother. "They're wild. Let the police handle them."

"I'm going to need one of Charlie's old shoes," said Dr. Ross. "I'll have to cut a hole for the big toe so Charlie can walk with this bandage on."

"Will you get his old blue sneaker?" Charlie's mother asked Encyclopedia. "It's in his closet."

"I'll be back in a wink," said Encyclopedia.

Leaving the doctor's office, the boy detective saw Duke Kelly, a Tiger, pacing the sidewalk. Duke looked worried.

Encyclopedia thought quickly. "Hey, Duke," he called. "You live near Charlie Stewart. Will you run to his house?"

"What for?"

"Charlie's been shot in the foot," said Encyclopedia. "The doctor wants to cut a hole in one of his shoes so he can walk around with the bandage on. Mrs. Stewart says to use one of his old blue sneakers. They're in his closet."

"Charlie's room is on the second floor in the front, isn't it?" said Duke. "All right, I guess I can find one of his blue sneakers."

When Duke returned with the sneaker, Encyclopedia took it to Dr. Ross. The doctor cut a hole in the sneaker for the wounded toe. Then he slipped the sneaker over Charlie's bandaged foot. It fit perfectly.

Immediately Encyclopedia marched outside.

"You're in a pack of trouble," he told Duke. "The Tigers have been secretly shooting a high-powered air gun in the ancient burial grounds. Now you've shot Charlie!"

"Me!" exclaimed Duke. "I didn't shoot anybody."

"You shot Charlie and followed us to the doctor's office. You were scared. So you waited around to learn how seriously Charlie was hurt."

"You're as nutty as a chestnut tree," retorted Duke. "I just happened to be standing here when you came out. I didn't know anything about Charlie being shot in the foot!"

"Yes, you did," said Encyclopedia. "Like every criminal, you made one mistake!"

WHAT WAS DUKE'S MISTAKE?

(Turn to page 109 for the solution to The Case of the Wounded Toe.)

The Case of Excalibur

Bugs Meany walked into the Brown Detective Agency. He placed twenty-five cents on the gasoline can.

"I want to hire you," he said.

Encyclopedia wasn't sure that he had heard right.

"The job I need done is hush-hush," the Tigers' leader muttered out of the corner of his mouth. "Undercover stuff, get me?"

"I'll keep it undercover. You won't know it from the inside of your bed," muttered back Encyclopedia. "What have you in mind?"

"I want you to get Excalibur."

"Is that worse than a sore throat?" said Encyclopedia.

"Excalibur is my new penknife," explained Bugs. "Remember Woody Fanfingle, the little squirt who beat me for the Idaville Mumblety-Peg championship last year? He just stole Excalibur."

"Why should he steal Excalibur?" asked Encyclopedia.

"Excalibur is a great knife," said Bugs. "Woody's afraid that with Excalibur I'll beat him this year."

"Are you certain it was Woody who stole the knife?"

"Fifteen minutes ago I found him sneaking about the Tigers' clubhouse," said Bugs. "He picked up Excalibur—it's a purple knife and my name is cut into it. He saw me and ran—we bumped as he got out the door. He shoved Excalibur into the pocket of his green pants as he got outside and kept running."

"You didn't chase him?"

"Naw, Woody broke his arm last week, and I don't fight one-armed kids," said Bugs. He rolled his eyes toward heaven. "Anyhow, his mother will be my math teacher next year."

"You want me to get the knife back without anyone knowing Woody stole it, is that the idea?" asked Encyclopedia.

"If Woody's mother hears I caught her son stealing, she'll hate me. I couldn't pass math next year in a flying saucer," said Bugs.

The Tigers' leader started for the garage door. "Woody is at the Little League game. Good luck, Brains, old boy."

Encyclopedia thought over the sly look on Bugs's face as he biked to Sally's house. He told her about the theft of Excalibur.

Sally stamped her foot. "Ooooh, that Bugs Meany!" she cried. "Don't trust him, Encyclopedia. Drop the case!"

"I don't trust Bugs any farther than I can throw a cheese cake under water," replied Encyclopedia. "Still, I'm in business. I take my customers as they come."

"But he *lied* to you," protested Sally. "Woody's mother isn't Mrs. Fanfingle, the math teacher. His mother is Mrs. Fanfingle, the lady barber on Watson Street. Bugs Meany is up to no good!"

"Then come along," said Encyclopedia. "I'll need you."

The two detectives rode their bikes behind the Idaville Elementary School. On the playground, the Little League game was underway.

Encyclopedia spied Charlie Stewart in the crowd. He asked Charlie to point out Woody Fanfingle.

Charlie pointed to an eight-year-old sitting on the bench. Although his broken left arm was held in a cast from his fingertips to above his elbow, Woody had on his baseball uniform.

"He gets dressed for every game," explained Charlie. "His teammates help him. They think he brings them good luck."

Encyclopedia returned to Sally. "I'm going down to the locker room," he said. "Stand by the door. Whistle if anyone approaches."

"I don't like this one bit," said Sally.

The locker room was empty. Encyclopedia went through each locker till he found one with a pair of green pants. The name Woody Fanfingle was sewn into the waistband.

Encyclopedia hesitated. Then, hearing no one, he quickly searched the pockets.

In the right pocket was a handkerchief, two stones, and a piece of string. In the left pocket was a penknife with "Bugs" cut into the purple handle—Excalibur!

As Encyclopedia slipped the knife into his pocket, a voice called, "Stop where you are!"

Mr. Evans and Bugs Meany suddenly appeared from the washroom. Mr. Evans was the school guard.

"Leroy Brown!" he exclaimed in astonishment. "So you're the boy who has been stealing from the lockers during the baseball games!"

Before Encyclopedia could answer, Bugs had rushed up. He pulled Excalibur from the boy detective's pocket.

"Why look, Mr. Evans," said Bugs. "It's my knife Excalibur—the one that Woody Fanfingle stole from the Tigers' clubhouse half an hour ago!"

Mr. Evans sent Bugs out to fetch Woody. A few moments later a grinning Bugs brought in a badly frightened Woody.

Mr. Evans questioned Woody sternly. Woody admitted that he had gone to the Tigers' clubhouse just before the game.

"I looked in at the door," said Woody. "I didn't see anyone. So I left and came over here and changed into my baseball uniform."

"He's lying like a carpet," sneered Bugs.

"So you're the boy who has been stealing!"

"I saw him put my knife into his left pants pocket as he ran from the Tigers' clubhouse. You saw Brown take it from the same pocket with your own eyes!"

"That I saw," agreed Mr. Evans, as Bugs fairly danced in glee.

"I owe you an apology," Mr. Evans said to Bugs. "Till you asked me to watch with you from the washroom, I had the idea *you* might be the locker room thief."

"Everybody suspects the worst of me," said Bugs righteously. "I don't mind. You got the real thief, Mr. Evans. And I got my knife back. That's all that matters."

Mr. Evans took Encyclopedia and Woody by the elbow.

"Come up to my office, boys," he said.

"Wait," said Encyclopedia. "Woody didn't steal Excalibur. Bugs planted it in his pants pocket while Woody was out on the field. Woody beat him in the Mumblety-Peg tournament last year, and Bugs wanted to get even."

"Next you'll be telling me I didn't see you trying to steal the knife out of the locker," said Mr. Evans.

"Bugs hired me to get the knife back," said Encyclopedia. "He's trying to get even with me, too. I can prove Excalibur was never stolen."

WHAT WAS THE PROOF?

*(Turn to page 110 for the solution to
The Case of Excalibur.)*

The Case of
the Glass of Ginger Ale

Chief Brown put down his cup of coffee. "Do you know anything about ginger ale?" he asked.

"It comes in a bottle, and I don't like it as much as root beer," answered Encyclopedia.

"What a strange question, dear," said Mrs. Brown, who was clearing away the dinner plates.

"It's a mighty strange case," replied Chief Brown. "Rafino de Verona is in the middle of it."

"Rafino de Verona!" exclaimed Encyclopedia. "The famous blind violinist?"

"Yes, he has a summer home on the beach," said Chief Brown. "He asked me to drop by this evening. He believes he's been tricked out of his prize violin by a glass of ginger ale."

With a whopper like that ringing in his ears, Encyclopedia could hardly stay in his chair. "Can I go with you, Dad?" he asked.

Chief Brown looked at Mrs. Brown.

"You may as well take him along," she said. "He may never again get a chance to meet someone like Rafino de Verona. But be home by nine-thirty."

Encyclopedia dashed to his room. He dug out his autograph book. When he reached the car, his father was waiting behind the wheel. Night was beginning to fall as they drove up to the house of the blind violinist.

A maid showed them into the living room. Mr. de Verona, a tall, white-haired man wearing dark glasses, came forward.

"Chief Brown," he said, holding out his hand. "You brought someone with you. Judging from the sound of sneakers, I should say a lad of ten or twelve."

"My son, Leroy," said Chief Brown. "He's ten."

"So nice of you to come, too, Leroy," said Mr. de Verona. He motioned father and son to chairs but remained standing himself.

"I'm almost too ashamed to tell you what happened," he said. "You'll think me a fool."

"Over the telephone you said you had lost your prize violin," said Chief Brown.

"Lost in a bet," said Mr. de Verona. "I made a bet last night with Hans Braun, concertmaster of the Glendon Symphony, and lost."

He crossed the room to a table. On the table was a tray, several glasses, an ice bucket, and three bottles of ginger ale. Encyclopedia marveled at how easily the sightless musician moved among the furniture.

"Clara, my maid, had the night off, and Hans Braun and I were alone in the house," said Mr. de Verona. "We sat in this room, and the talk soon moved from music to mysteries. Hans is especially interested in locked room puzzles. Almost before I knew it, I'd bet my Stradivarius violin against his Stradivarius."

Mr. de Verona ran his fine, strong fingers through his mop of white hair. "I didn't think I could lose! Hans positively worked a miracle to win!"

The blind musician reached into the ice bucket. He dropped four pieces of ice into a tall glass.

"Hans said, 'Oh, this ice is cold,' as he filled a glass with four pieces of ice, just as I have done," said Mr. de Verona. "Then Hans gave me the glass to hold. I heard him open a bottle of ginger ale. He left the room carrying it."

Mr. de Verona, glass in hand, went to the door of the living room and locked it.

"I locked the door after making sure that Hans was out in the hall. Next I locked the two windows."

Mr. de Verona went about locking the two windows. One was behind the piano, the other behind Chief Brown's chair. Now there was no way of getting into the living room without breaking the windows or door.

Mr. de Verona strode across the room. He stopped at an oil painting hanging on the wall and pushed it aside. Behind the painting was a wall safe.

"I felt in Hans's glass to make sure it was

filled only with ice," he said. "Then I put the glass with the ice inside the safe and locked the safe."

Mr. de Verona locked the safe and replaced the oil painting. He walked to the door and switched off the lights.

For a second the lone sound was the ticking of the grandfather clock by the bookcase.

Mr. de Verona's voice came from the darkness.

"The bet was that I was to sit in an easy chair in the middle of the room. I was to stay seated exactly one hour. In that hour, Hans was to enter the locked, lightless room, open the locked safe, take out the glass, remove the ice, pour into the glass the bottle of ginger ale he had carried into the hall, lock the safe, leave the room, and lock the door behind him—*all without my hearing him!*"

Mr. de Verona sat down in an easy chair in the center of the dark room.

"I can tell time by the raised numbers on my wrist watch," the blind musician said. "After an hour had passed, I had heard nothing. I was sure I had the bet won. I

"I put the glass with ice inside the safe."

unlocked the door and kept Hans talking in the hall so that I should know where he was. I crossed the room and opened the safe. The glass was still there. The ice was gone. Instead, the glass was filled—by thunder!—with ginger ale! I tasted it!"

Mr. de Verona slapped the arms of his chair in bewilderment. "How did Hans do it?" he cried.

For a long moment the room was still. Finally Mr. de Verona arose and switched on the lights.

Chief Brown looked questioningly at Encyclopedia. "Any ideas?" his eyes asked.

Encyclopedia nodded. "May I ask a question, sir?"

"Please do, Leroy," said Mr. de Verona.

"Who brought up the subject of locked rooms?" asked the boy detective.

"Why, now that I think about it, I suppose it was Hans," answered Mr. de Verona. "What is the difference? What I want to know is why I didn't hear him?"

"There is nothing wrong with your hearing, sir," said Encyclopedia. "No man could have heard the second clue."

He picked up his autograph book. "Would you please sign this for me?"

ENCYCLOPEDIA KNEW HOW HANS HAD FILLED THE GLASS IN THE SAFE WITH GINGER ALE. DO YOU?

(Turn to page 111 for the solution to The Case of the Glass of Ginger Ale.)

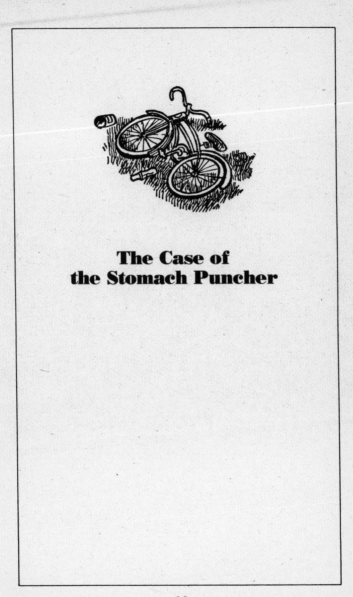

The Case of
the Stomach Puncher

It was very unusual for Herb Stein to *walk* into the Brown Detective Agency.

Herb was Idaville's junior bicycle champion. Usually he came riding up at top speed. He was the only boy in town who wore out the seat of his pants before his sneakers.

"Who grounded you?" asked Encyclopedia.

"Biff Logan," answered the walking Herb. He rolled twenty-five cents onto the gasoline can. "Biff stole my bicycle."

Encyclopedia gave the money some

thought. Herb was one of his best pals . . .

"Go on, take it," urged Herb. "You'll earn it."

"Is this case dangerous?"

"Only around the belt line," said Herb. "You've heard of Biff Logan. If he doesn't like you, he smacks you in the belly, pow!"

"Biff won't exactly kiss me if I accuse him of stealing your bike," observed the boy detective. He pictured Biff Logan in action. Suddenly twenty-five cents wasn't nearly enough to charge Herb.

"Last week Biff tangled with three of Bugs Meany's Tigers," said Herb. "He smacked them each in the stomach—*biff, bam, sock!* They couldn't eat for a day and a half."

"I'd better not tell Sally about this case," mused Encyclopedia. "She might try to mix with Biff. He's too old and too big for her. We'll have to outsmart him."

"If you don't," warned Herb, "he'll smack you in the belly, *pow!*"

"I heard you the first time," said Encyclopedia. "Give me the facts."

"Yesterday my bike was stolen from in front of my house," said Herb. "Nancy Etzwiler, who lives down the block, thinks she saw Biff riding it. I went to Biff's house. He was busy in the back yard covering something with a big canvas."

"You felt it was unwise to accuse him then and there?"

Herb rubbed his belly and nodded.

Encyclopedia poked around in the rear of the garage. He found a strip of sheet metal on a shelf. He lowered his pants. With the rope from his kite, he tied the sheet metal around his waist. Then he pulled up his pants to cover the armor.

"You look like an overstuffed can of beans," said Herb.

"I don't care if I look like I ate a sofa so long as Biff Logan calls me Fatso," said Encyclopedia. "I'm counting on the fact that he never saw me before, fat or slim."

Because of the sheet metal middle, Encyclopedia wobbled rather than walked. He couldn't bend at the waist. He had to bend his knees in order to pick up a baseball and bat.

"We'll need these," he said. "We can get into Biff's back yard if we pretend to chase a baseball."

Herb pedalled Encyclopedia's bike while the punch-proof sleuth sat on the cross bar. Biff's house was in the old, run-down part of town beside an empty lot.

The two friends got off the bike and began hitting the ball in the empty lot. Four times Herb hit the ball into Biff's back yard. Four times Biff stormed out of the house. He threw the ball back with an angry warning.

"He's the toughest sixteen-year-old kid in Idaville," said Herb gloomily. "Why did he pick *my* bike to steal?"

"Keep a good grip on the bat," Encyclopedia ordered. "We're moving in!"

Encyclopedia took aim and threw the ball at the lump of canvas behind Biff's house. Then the two boys hurried through Biff's back yard jungle of old tires, bed-springs, screens, and cement blocks.

Encyclopedia picked up the ball. He was lifting one corner of the canvas when Biff charged out.

"Get away from there, Blimp!" shouted Biff, shaking his fist in Encyclopedia's face.

"You know what I'm going to give you two smart guys?" asked Biff. "The same thing I give all snoopers—a punch in the eye."

"A punch in t-the *e-eye?*" stammered Herb.

"Don't you mean the belly?" said Encyclopedia weakly. "I'm sure you mean the belly."

"The eye," said Biff. "The last kid I punched in the belly couldn't eat for a week. He nearly starved to death."

Herb dropped the bat. He sagged to the ground.

Biff grabbed Encyclopedia by the collar.

"Go ahead, give me a black eye," said Encyclopedia. "Let everybody see where you punched a smaller boy. How stupid can you get?"

Biff hesitated. "You got something there," he said. "The old way was better. No marks—so no proof."

"Don't spare me," said Encyclopedia with a noble lift of his chin. "I'll take my medicine like a man."

"The pleasure is all mine," said Biff, swinging for the stomach.

Flesh and bone met sheet metal.

Encyclopedia was knocked backward seven feet.

"*Ye-o-ow!*" screamed Biff. "Yipe! Yipe! Yipe!"

Encyclopedia was knocked backward.

Herb quickly pulled back the canvas. Underneath was a shiny red bicycle. It lay on its side on the green grass.

"Yours?" Encyclopedia asked.

"It looks like my bike, but I can't be sure," said Herb. "I only got it two days ago. I didn't have a chance to put my name on it yet."

"You mean it might not be yours?" Encyclopedia gazed uneasily at Biff. The big boy was rolling on the ground in pain.

"What do you eat, Blimp, nails?" groaned Biff, shaking his hurt hand.

"You stole this bike yesterday, confess!" said Encyclopedia.

"You're crazy," grunted Biff. "It's been here under the canvas ever since I bought it two months ago."

"Maybe it's all a terrible mistake," whispered Herb. "Biff still has a good left hand. Let's get out of here while we can still walk."

"We're pedaling out—both of us," said Encyclopedia. "There's been no mistake. Biff stole your bike all right."

HOW DID ENCYCLOPEDIA KNOW?

(Turn to page 112 for the solution to The Case of the Stomach Puncher.)

Solution to *The Case of the Secret Pitch*

Encyclopedia knew instantly that neither the letter nor the check was written by the Yankee pitcher, Spike Browning, nor by any grown-up.

Both the check and the letter bore the same date—June 31, but no year was given.

And there is no June 31. June has only 30 days!

Shown the errors, Bugs could do nothing but admit having written the letter and check himself. As the loser of the bet, he had to give Speedy Flanagan his baseball bat.

Solution to *The Case of the Balloon Man*

Mr. Potts overlooked the fact that Izzy always blew up his green and pink balloons with his mouth. That is, the balloons had nothing but breath, or air, in them. Balloons with nothing but air in them do not rise high into a tree on a day without breeze. They sink to earth!

(Only a balloon blown up with something lighter than air—such as helium—will rise high into the air.)

Encyclopedia immediately realized that Mr. Potts had planted the balloon in the tree ahead of time. Then he had told the Reverend he had just seen it.

This gave Mr. Potts the chance to climb up the ladder. Looking over the twelve-foot wall, he pretended to see Izzy kidnapping little Bobby.

Encyclopedia knew that Mr. Potts must have kidnapped both Izzy and Bobby at some earlier time.

When Chief Brown heard this, he went to Mr. Potts's house. He found Bobby and Izzy tied up. Izzy's truck was hidden in Mr. Potts's garage.

Caught, Mr. Potts confessed. He had rented the house behind the Tylers' in order to kidnap Bobby and hold him for the ransom money.

Solution to *The Case of the Ambushed Cowboy*

Ringo Charlie had said Johnny Kid knew he was coming because at nine o'clock in the morning, his shadow, falling *ahead* of him, gave him away.

Johnny Kid had seen the shadow and jumped from behind the rock, shooting.

But Mr. Scotty, the guide, acting out the part of Ringo Charlie at the same time and on the same spot, had "squinted into the morning sun."

That proved Ringo Charlie lied.

With the sun in his face, Ringo Charlie's shadow would have fallen *behind* him!

Solution to *The Case of the Forgetful Sheriff*

Mr. Baker said:

"You can't shoot seven bullets from a six-gun." Count them.

Sheriff Wiggins claimed: he was wounded in the left arm by two shots (two bullets) from the lookout's six-gun; he then seized the lookout's gun and killed him with it (three bullets); then he shot the remaining four outlaws (seven bullets!).

Encyclopedia reasoned (as had Mr. Baker) that the sheriff was secretly a member of the holdup gang. In riding after his outlaw partners, the lawman didn't bother to put on his gun because he didn't think he'd need it.

Then he had a falling out over the division of the loot, probably. Getting hold of a gun, he surprised and killed his partners.

Before he could ride off with the gold, the posse reached him. So he had to make up the story about shooting the five outlaws in the line of duty.

Solution to *The Case of the Hungry Hitchhiker*

The hitchhiker made his mistake by trying to be friendly. He never should have given the boy detective the chocolate bar.

Encyclopedia had to "break off" two squares. That meant the chocolate was *hard*. But the hitchhiker had said he was waiting at the crossroads for "about an hour" on a hot day when the temperature had reached "ninety-three" degrees.

Had the hitchhiker been telling the truth, the chocolate bar would have melted in the heat. Instead of being *hard*, it would have been like *soup*.

The hitchhiker could only have had one reason for lying. He had to be a member of the holdup gang who was left behind to direct pursuit away from the road that the getaway car had really taken!

The fake hitchhiker confessed that he kept the knapsack in the air-conditioned getaway car till it was time for him to act out his part.

The entire gang was quickly rounded up.

Solution to *The Case of the Two-Fisted Poet*

Before the fight, Percy had placed his eyeglasses in "the breast pocket" of his suitcoat.

During the fight, the bigger boy pounded Percy's "chest" and stomach with body blows.

Yet after the fight Percy had put on his eyeglasses again.

That was Percy's mistake!

Had the bigger boy hit Percy as hard as he could, Percy's eyeglasses—lenses and frames—would have been smashed by the body blows.

Encyclopedia knew, therefore, that the bigger boy was faking his punches. He was helping Percy show off in front of Sally!

Solution to *The Case of the Wounded Toe*

Duke told Encyclopedia that he "didn't know anything about Charlie being shot in the foot."

But he gave himself away by not asking *which* sneaker he should bring from Charlie's closet.

When Dr. Ross cut a hole for the wounded toe in Charlie's sneaker, "It fit perfectly."

That meant Duke had brought the left sneaker.

Yet he couldn't know whether to bring the left or the right sneaker unless he had seen the wound.

When Chief Brown told this to Duke's parents, Duke confessed. He said he had not meant to hit Charlie, only to scare him away from the Tigers' secret firing range.

The police took the air gun from the Tigers.

And each boy's parents punished him for holding target practice in the ancient burial grounds.

Solution to *The Case of Excalibur*

Bugs's own words to Mr. Evans proved he had not seen Woody steal the penknife as he claimed.

Bugs had said:

"I saw him put my knife Excalibur into his left pants pocket as he ran from the Tigers' clubhouse. You saw Brown take it from the same pocket with your own eyes!"

Now Woody had broken his left arm. It was "in a cast from his fingertips to above his elbow."

Therefore Woody could not have used his left hand to slip the penknife into his pocket. He would have had to use his right hand.

But Excalibur was found in his *left* pocket.

Try to put a penknife into your left pants pocket with your right hand while running.

It's impossible.

If Woody had stolen Excalibur, he would have put it in his *right* pants pocket.

Solution to *The Case of the Glass of Ginger Ale*

The *first* clue was Hans's remark, "Oh, this ice is cold."

It was a silly, obvious thing to say. It made sense only if it covered up another sound he didn't want the blind violinist to hear.

Encyclopedia reasoned that the other sound was Hans tearing open an insulated bag—the kind of bag which keeps ice from melting.

Yes, Hans had brought his own ice. He did not take the four pieces of ice from Mr. de Verona's ice bucket.

The pieces of ice in the glass which Mr. de Verona put in the safe were not made of water.

Hans had made them by freezing ginger ale!

Hans never did open the safe. He never even entered the room. He simply waited in the hall for an hour.

The *second* clue, the one "no man could have heard," was the sound of the frozen pieces of ginger ale melting.

When Mr. de Verona opened the safe, the pieces of ice had all melted, filling the glass with ginger ale!

Solution to *The Case of the Stomach Puncher*

Biff said that the bike had been lying "under the canvas ever since I bought it two months ago."

Yet when Encyclopedia removed the canvas, the bike lay on grass that was "green."

Had the canvas been covering the bike and the ground for two months, the grass would have died.

Dead grass is brown, not green.

The green, live grass proved the canvas had just been put over the ground and the bike.

ABOUT THE AUTHOR

Since the publication of the first *Encyclopedia Brown* book in 1963, DONALD J. SOBOL has written roughly one book a year. In 1967, at a Children's Book Fair, he explained, "I began writing children's mysteries because the mystery element was really very small in the so-called mysteries that were written for children and I felt that this was a shame." In 1976, the Encyclopedia Brown series was the recipient of a special 1976 Edgar Allan Poe Award, presented by the Mystery Writers of America in recognition of these books as the first mysteries that millions of children read. In addition to the Encyclopedia Brown series, Mr. Sobol has authored over twenty books for young readers. A native of New York, he now lives in Florida with his wife and children. He has been a free-lance writer for eighteen years.

Match Wits with America's
Sherlock Holmes in
Sneakers

ENCYCLOPEDIA BROWN

With a head full of facts and his
eyes and ears on the world of
Idaville, meet Leroy (Encyclopedia) Brown. Each Encyclopedia Brown book contains 10 baf-
fling cases to challenge, stymie
and amuse young sleuths. Best of
all, the reader can try solving
each case on his own before
looking up the solution in the
back of the book. "BRIGHT
AND ENTERTAINING. . . ."
The New York Times
By Donald Sobol

☐ 15359	ENCYCLOPEDIA BROWN BOY DETECTIVE #1	$2.25
☐ 15392	ENCYCLOPEDIA BROWN/CASE OF THE SECRET PITCH #2	$2.25
☐ 15177	ENCYCLOPEDIA BROWN FINDS THE CLUE #3	$2.25
☐ 15411	ENCYCLOPEDIA BROWN GETS HIS MAN #4	$2.25
☐ 15404	ENCYCLOPEDIA BROWN KEEPS THE PEACE #6	$2.25
☐ 15389	ENCYCLOPEDIA BROWN SAVES THE DAY #7	$2.25
☐ 15410	ENCYCLOPEDIA BROWN TRACKS THEM DOWN #8	$2.25
☐ 15393	ENCYCLOPEDIA BROWN SHOWS THE WAY #9	$2.25
☐ 15423	ENCYCLOPEDIA BROWN TAKES THE CASE #10	$2.25
☐ 15371	ENCYCLOPEDIA BROWN & THE CASE OF THE MIDNIGHT VISITOR #13	$2.25
☐ 15352	ENCYCLOPEDIA BROWN AND THE MYSTERIOUS HANDPRINTS #16	$2.25

Prices and availability subject to change without notice.

Buy them at your local bookstore or use this handy coupon for ordering:

More Fun More Adventure More Magic

☐ **15348 DANCING CATS OF APPLESAP**
by Janet Taylor Lisle   **$2.50**
Only Melba Morris, age 10, knows that the 100 wondrous cats who
dance the days away in Mr. Jiggs' drugstore are really . . . a miracle.

☐ **15350 OWLS IN THE FAMILY**
by Farley Mowat   **$2.25**
There's nothing two owls named Wol and Weeps can't do—from
turning the whole household topsy-turvy to shaking up the entire
neighborhood!

☐ **21129 THE WIND IN THE WILLOWS**
by Kenneth Grahame   **$1.95**
When Rat and Mole and Badger and Toad get together for a series
of outrageously silly adventures, the fun never stops.

☐ **15349 THE OWLSTONE CROWN**
by X. J. Kennedy   **$2.50**
When Timothy and Verity Tibbs follow a tiny ladybug private eye
over a moon-lit path to Other Earth, magical adventures happen
fast.

☐ **15317 JAMES AND THE GIANT PEACH**
by Roald Dahl   **$2.95**
James, sadly resigned to a life of misery with two wicked aunts,
rolls instead into a truly wild adventure . . . inside a giant magical
peach!

You can order these books today.

Prices and availability subject to change without notice.

CHOOSE YOUR OWN ADVENTURE

SKYLARK EDITIONS

☐ 15480	The Green Slime #6 S. Saunders	$2.25
☐ 15195	Help! You're Shrinking #7 E. Packard	$1.95
☐ 15496	Indian Trail #8 R. A. Montgomery	$2.25
☐ 15506	Dream Trips #9 E. Packard	$2.25
☐ 15495	The Genie In the Bottle #10 J. Razzi	$2.25
☐ 15222	The Big Foot Mystery #11 L. Sonberg	$1.95
☐ 15424	The Creature From Miller's Pond #12 S. Saunders	$2.25
☐ 15226	Jungle Safari #13 E. Packard	$1.95
☐ 15442	The Search For Champ #14 S. Gilligan	$2.25
☐ 15444	Three Wishes #15 S. Gilligan	$2.25
☐ 15465	Dragons! #16 J. Razzi	$2.25
☐ 15489	Wild Horse Country #17 L. Sonberg	$2.25
☐ 15262	Summer Camp #18 J. Gitenstein	$1.95
☐ 15490	The Tower of London #19 S. Saunders	$2.25
☐ 15501	Trouble In Space #20 J. Woodcock	$2.25
☐ 15283	Mona Is Missing #21 S. Gilligan	$1.95
☐ 15418	The Evil Wizard #22 A. Packard	$2.25
☐ 15305	The Flying Carpet #25 J. Razzi	$1.95
☐ 15318	The Magic Path #26 J. Goodman	$1.95
☐ 15467	Ice Cave #27 Saunders, Packard	$2.25
☐ 15342	The Fairy Kidnap #29 S. Gilligan	$1.95
☐ 25463	Runaway Spaceship #30 S. Saunders	$2.25
☐ 15508	Lost Dog! #31 R. A. Montgomery	$2.25
☐ 15379	Blizzard of Black Swan #32 Saunders/Packard	$2.25
☐ 15380	Haunted Harbor #33 S. Gilligan	$2.25
☐ 15399	Attack of the Monster Plants #34 S. Saunders	$2.25

Prices and availability subject to change without notice.

Shop at home
for quality childrens books
and save money, too.

Now you can order books for the whole family from Bantam's latest listing of hundreds of titles including many fine children's books. *And* this special offer gives you an opportunity to purchase a Bantam book for only 50¢. Here's how:

By ordering any five books at the regular price per order, you can also choose any other single book listed (up to $4.95 value) for just 50¢. Some restrictions do apply, so for further details send for Bantam's listing of titles today.

Here are more of the "kid-pleasing" paperbacks that everyone loves.

- ☐ 15272 **YOU'RE GOING OUT THERE A KID AND COMING BACK A STAR** L. Hirsch $2.25
- ☐ 15260 **SEBASTIAN SUPER SLEUTH & HAIR OF THE DOG MYSTERY** M. Christian $2.25
- ☐ 15382 **SHERLUCK BONES MYSTERY DETECTIVE BOOK #1** J. & M. Razzi $2.25
- ☐ 15118 **SHERLUCK BONES MYSTERY DETECTIVE BOOK #2** J. & M. Razzi $1.95
- ☐ 15197 **SHERLUCK BONES MYSTERY DETECTIVE BOOK #3** J. & M. Razzi $1.95
- ☐ 15210 **SHERLUCK BONES MYSTERY DETECTIVE BOOK #4** J. & M. Razzi $1.95
- ☐ 15425 **SHERLUCK BONES MYSTERY DETECTIVE BOOK #5** J. & M. Razzi $2.25
- ☐ 15412 **SHERLUCK BONES MYSTERY DETECTIVE BOOK #6** J. & M. Razzi $2.25
- ☐ 15187 **DETECTIVE POUFY'S FIRST CASE** C. Pomerantz $1.95
- ☐ 15394 **GEORGE'S MARVELOUS MEDICINE** $2.50
- ☐ 15350 **OWLS IN THE FAMILY** F. Mowat $2.25
- ☐ 15390 **FANTASTIC MR. FOX** R. Dahl $2.50
- ☐ 15289 **DANNY THE CHAMPION OF THE WORLD** R. Dahl $2.50

Prices and availability subject to change without notice.

JIM KJELGAARD

In these adventure stories, Jim Kjelgaard shows us the special world of animals, the wilderness, and the bonds between men and dogs. *Irish Red* and *Outlaw Red* are stories about two champion Irish setters. *Snow Dog* shows what happens when a half-wild dog crosses paths with a trapper. The cougar-hunting *Lion Hound* and the greyhound story *Desert Dog* take place in our present-day Southwest. And, *Stormy* is an extraordinary story of a boy and his devoted dog. You'll want to read all these exciting books.

☐ 15456	A NOSE FOR TROUBLE	$2.50
☐ 15368	HAUNT FOX	$2.25
☐ 15434	BIG RED	$2.95
☐ 15324	DESERT DOG	$2.50
☐ 15286	IRISH RED: SON OF BIG RED	$2.50
☐ 15427	LION HOUND	$2.95
☐ 15339	OUTLAW RED	$2.50
☐ 15365	SNOW DOG	$2.50
☐ 15388	STORMY	$2.50
☐ 15466	WILD TREK	$2.75

Prices and availability subject to change without notice.